A Day With

A Day With

ICONIC SCIENTISTS

MOONSTONE

Published in Moonstone
by Rupa Publications India Pvt. Ltd 2023
7/16, Ansari Road, Daryaganj
New Delhi 110002

Sales centres:
Prayagraj Bengaluru Chennai
Hyderabad Jaipur Kathmandu
Kolkata Mumbai

P-ISBN: 978-93-5520-920-7
E-ISBN: 978-93-5520-921-4

First impression 2023

10 9 8 7 6 5 4 3 2 1

Printed in India

Contents

Marie Curie

Benjamin Franklin

Louis Pasteur

Thomas Alva Edison

Marie Curie

Marie Curie made many important discoveries.
What were these discoveries?
Why were they so important?
Read on to discover the answer.

Meet Tim and Tyra

Hi, I'm Tim.

Hi, I'm Tyra. We are going to travel back in time to visit Marie Curie. Let's meet her now.

Marie Curie was born on 7 November, 1867 in Warsaw, **Poland**.
Her name when she was born was Maria Sklodowska.
She became a great **scientist**.

Maria's parents were teachers.
They taught Maria that learning was fun.
Maria loved school. She was the best student in her class.
Her school gave her a gold medal.

When Maria finished high school, she became a teacher. At night, she read books about science. Maria loved science. She wanted to learn more and more.

Maria went to a **university** in **France**.
She studied math and science at the university.

Chapter 3: Two Scientists

While she was in France, Maria met a scientist.
His name was Pierre Curie.
They fell in love and got married.
Maria changed her name to Marie Curie.
Marie and Pierre worked on science projects together.

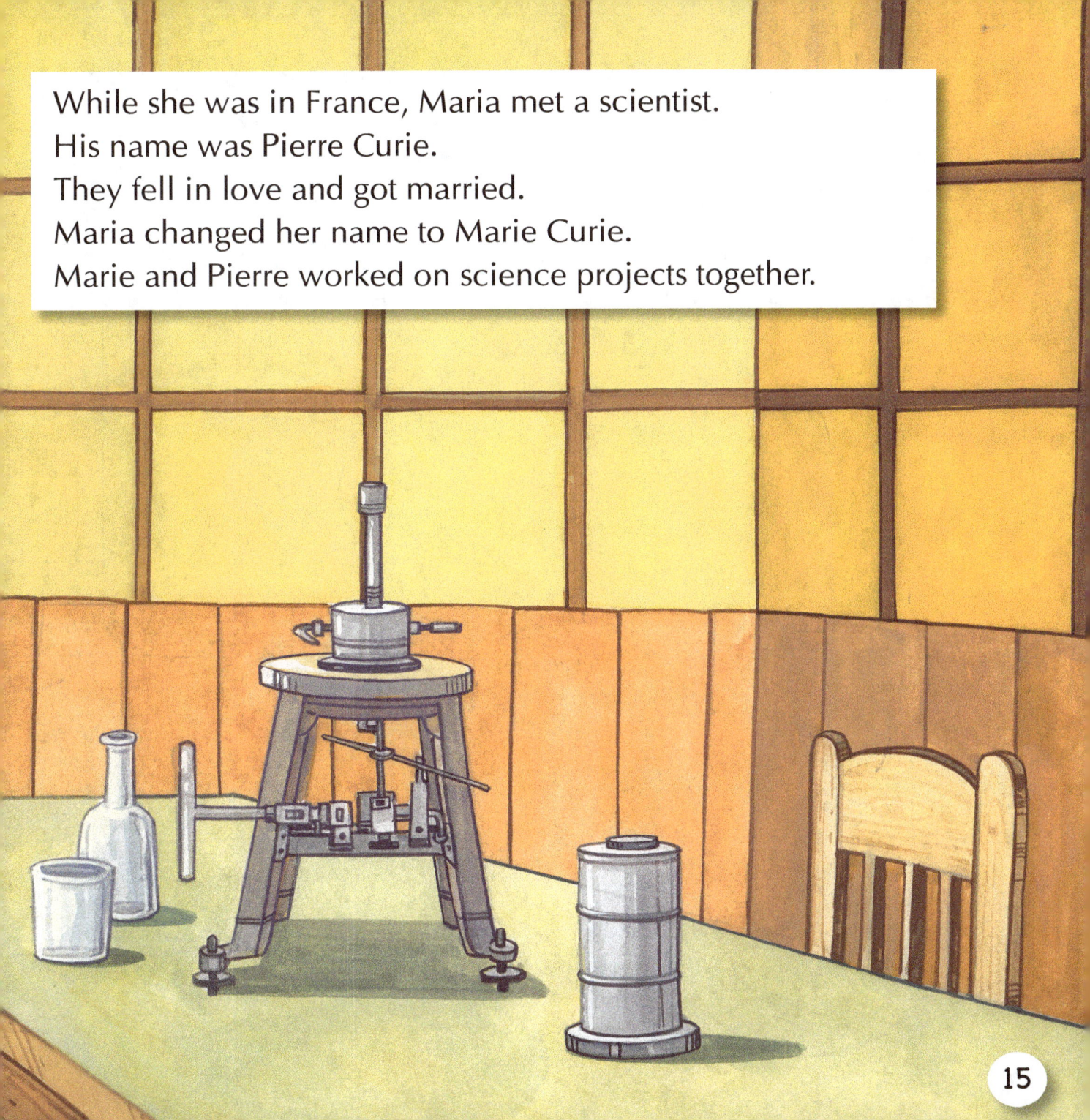

Chapter 4: Strong Rays

Marie Curie learned about the work of another scientist.
This scientist had discovered strange **rays.**
These rays were not bright, but they were powerful.
These rays were called **X rays.**
X rays can pass through skin.
X rays can be used to take pictures of bones in the human body.

Marie wanted to learn all about these special rays.

Chapter 5: Uranium

Marie and Pierre had a friend named Henri Becquerel. Becquerel studied a metal called **uranium**.

Becquerel discovered that uranium gave off rays. The rays were like X rays, but not as strong. They could go through paper, but not skin.

Marie studied uranium to learn more about these rays. She called the energy that came from the rays **'radioactivity'**.

Uranium is an **element**.
Everything in nature is made out of elements.
Gold and iron are also examples of elements.

Marie Curie wanted to find out what other elements gave off rays. Marie and Pierre Curie worked together. They discovered new elements. One of these elements was **radium**.

Radium gives off very strong rays.
These rays can be used to cure people who are sick with **cancer**. The rays can also be used to cure other sicknesses.

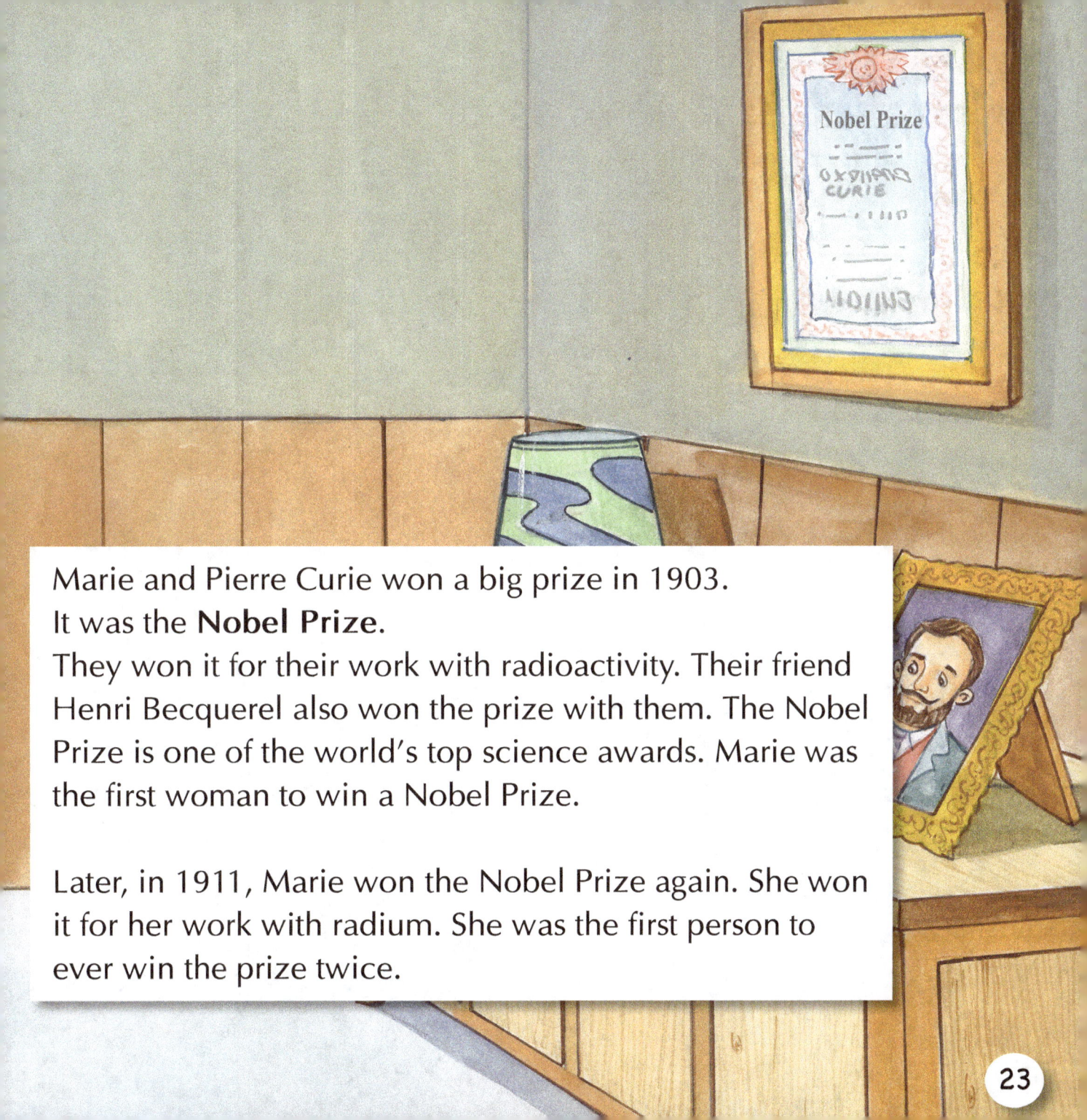

Marie and Pierre Curie won a big prize in 1903.
It was the **Nobel Prize**.
They won it for their work with radioactivity. Their friend Henri Becquerel also won the prize with them. The Nobel Prize is one of the world's top science awards. Marie was the first woman to win a Nobel Prize.

Later, in 1911, Marie won the Nobel Prize again. She won it for her work with radium. She was the first person to ever win the prize twice.

After Marie Curie won her first Nobel Prize, she became a professor.
A professor is a teacher at a university.
Marie was a professor at the Sorbonne University in France.
She was the first woman to teach at a university in France.

Marie Curie was an important scientist.
She discovered new things.
And she showed that women could be great scientists too.

Marie Curie died in Passy, France on 4 July, 1934.

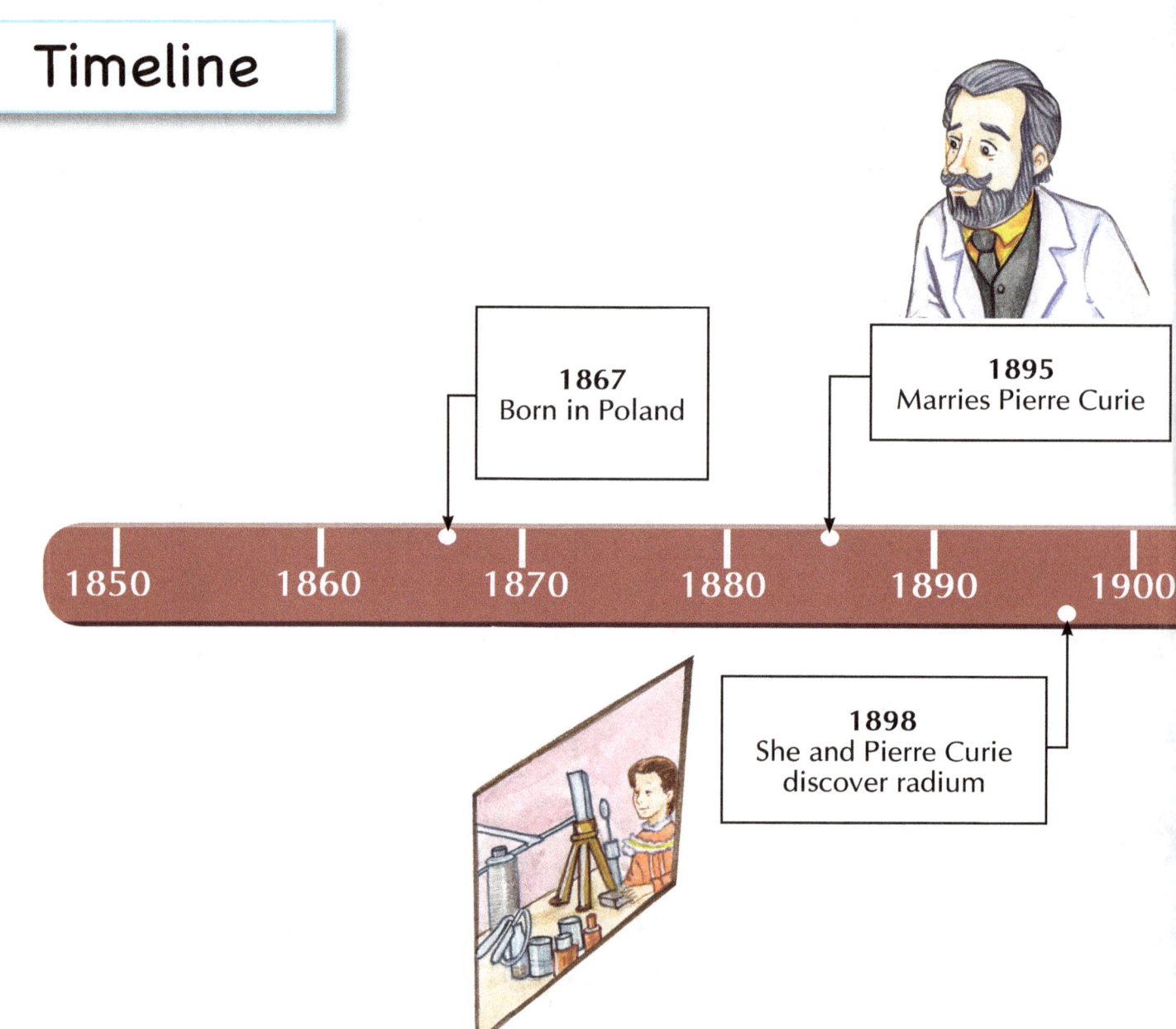

1867
Born in Poland

1895
Marries Pierre Curie

1850   1860   1870   1880   1890   1900

1898
She and Pierre Curie
discover radium

Marie Curie's Life and Work

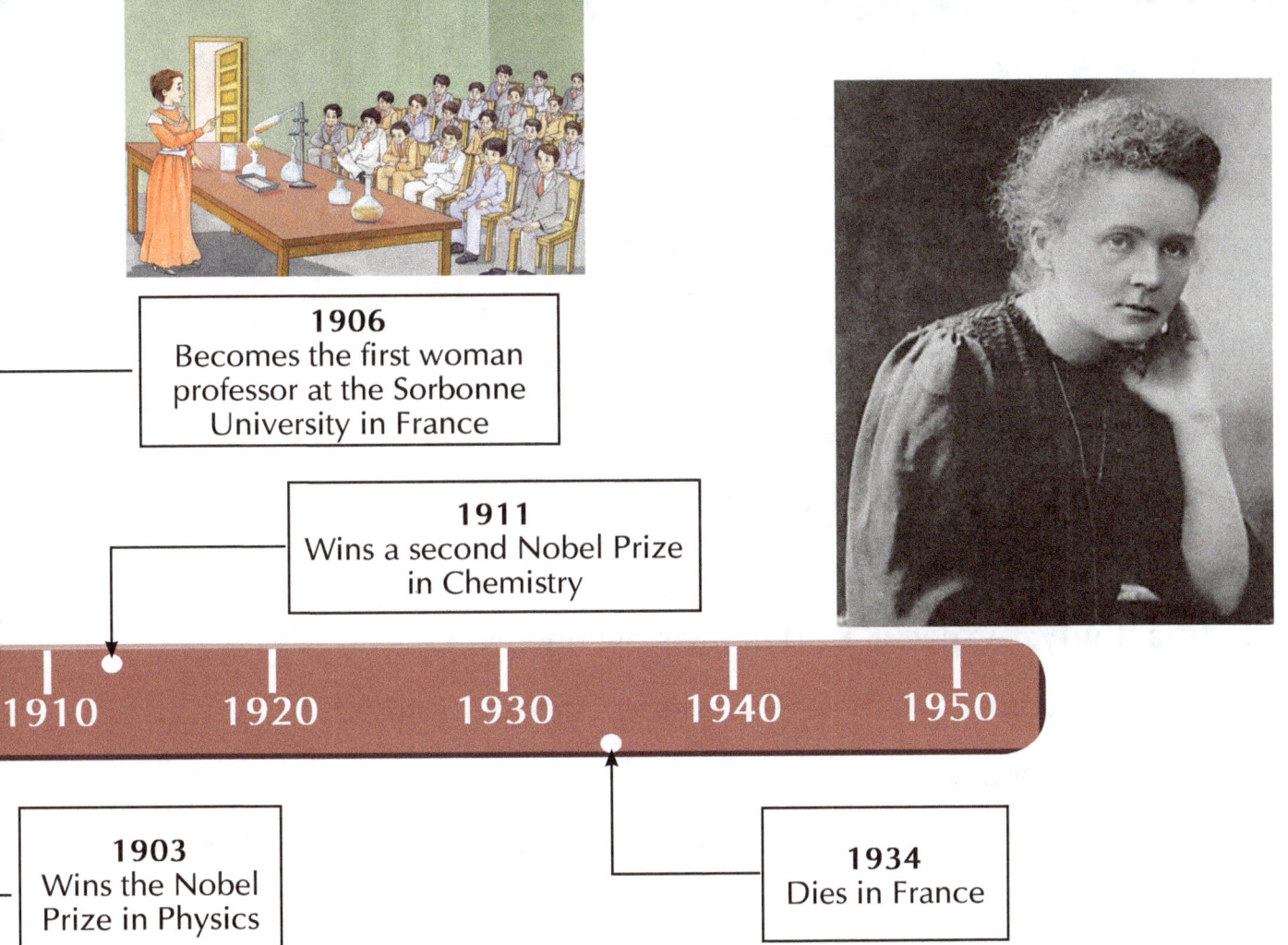

1906
Becomes the first woman professor at the Sorbonne University in France

1911
Wins a second Nobel Prize in Chemistry

1910   1920   1930   1940   1950

1903
Wins the Nobel Prize in Physics

1934
Dies in France

Word Meanings

Cancer: A disease that makes people very sick

Element: The basic material or substance that makes up everything in the world. There are over 100 known elements

France: A country in western Europe

Nobel Prize: A special prize that recognizes great work

Poland: A country in the middle of Europe

Radioactivity: A special kind of invisible energy

Radium: A radioactive metal that Marie Curie discovered

Rays: Beams of energy

Scientist: A person who studies science to learn and discover things

University: A school you go to after you have finished high school

Uranium: A radioactive metal that Marie Curie studied

X rays: Rays that can pass through things that ordinary light cannot pass though. X rays can pass through skin. They can be used to take pictures of parts of the body that cannot be seen from the outside

Think, Talk and Write

Think About It

Read Chapter 1 again.
How did Marie Curie's early years help her become a scientist?
Write a list of things that helped her become a scientist.

Talk About It

What interests you most about Marie?
Tell a classmate about her.
Explain to a classmate what interests you most about her.

Write About It

Marie learned a lot about X rays and how they work.
How do people use X rays today?
Write a letter to Marie telling her how and why people use X rays today.

What did you learn from Marie Curie?

....

....

....

....

....

....

....

....

....

....

....

....

....

....

....

What are the five things that you will change after reading Marie Curie's story?

....

....

....

....

....

....

....

....

....

....

....

....

....

....

Benjamin Franklin

Benjamin Franklin invented many things.
What were these inventions?
Why were they so important?
Read on to discover the answer.

Meet Tim and Tyra

Hi, I'm Tim.

Hi, I'm Tyra. We are going to travel back in time to visit Benjamin Franklin. Let's meet him now.

Benjamin Franklin was born in Boston, **USA** on 17 January, 1706. He was a great leader. He was also a scientist and **inventor**.

In Benjamin Franklin's time, most fireplaces did not make the whole room warm.
He wanted to make a better fireplace.
He invented a special stove.
This stove was not used for cooking.
It was a new kind of fireplace.
It sat in the middle of the room.
The whole room got warm.
It was called the **Franklin stove**.

In Benjamin Franklin's time, people did not know very much about **electricity**.
Electricity is a kind of energy. Franklin thought lightning might have electricity.
How could he find out?

Franklin made a kite. He put a wire on the top of it, attached a string to the kite and tied a metal key to the end of the string.

Franklin flew his kite in a thunderstorm. Lightning hit the kite. The electricity from the lightning went down the string to the key. Franklin felt a shock from the electricity. He was right. Lightning does have electricity.

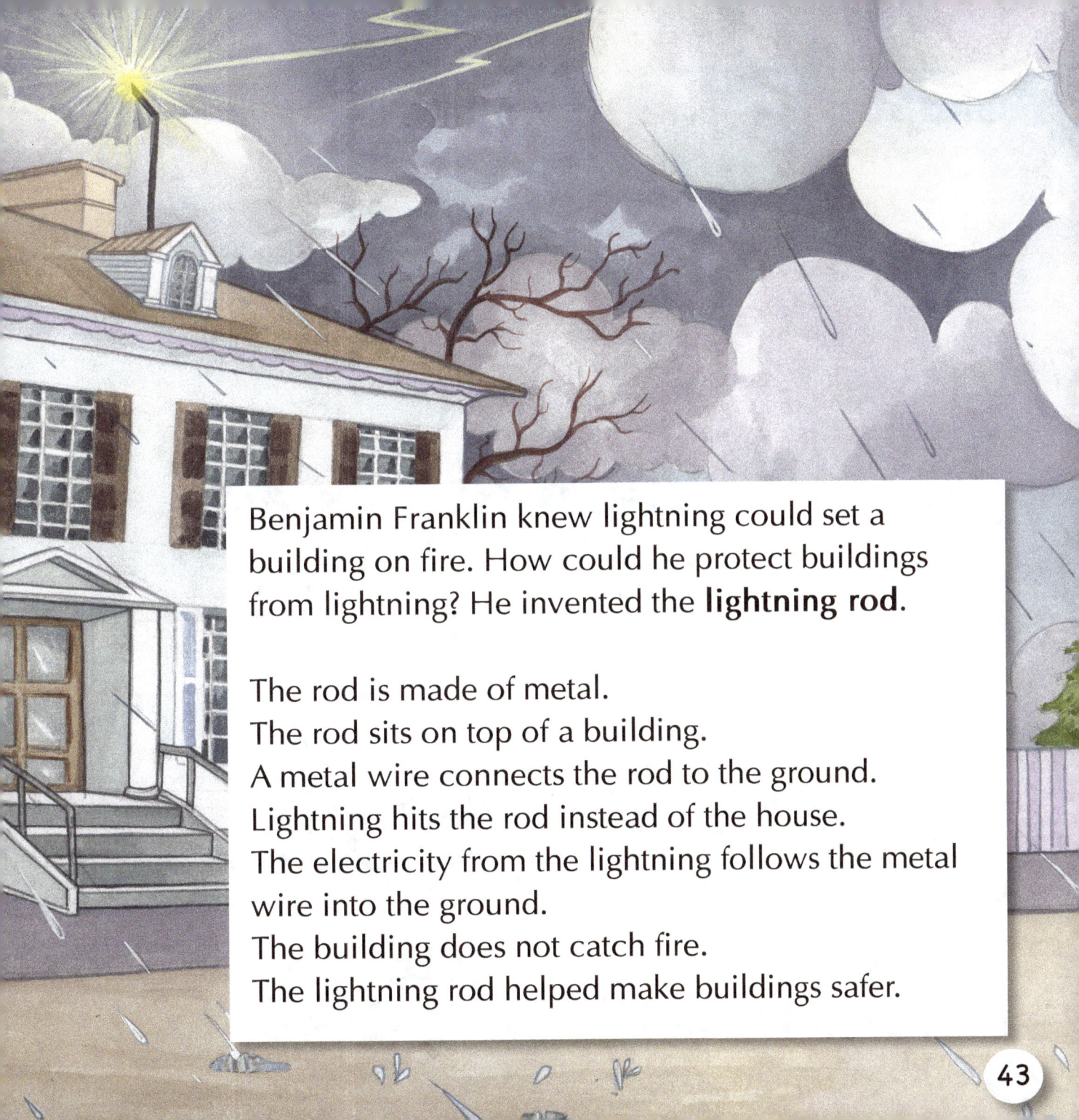

Benjamin Franklin knew lightning could set a building on fire. How could he protect buildings from lightning? He invented the **lightning rod**.

The rod is made of metal.
The rod sits on top of a building.
A metal wire connects the rod to the ground.
Lightning hits the rod instead of the house.
The electricity from the lightning follows the metal wire into the ground.
The building does not catch fire.
The lightning rod helped make buildings safer.

Benjamin Franklin loved music. He could play many instruments. He could play the guitar and the violin. Could he invent a new instrument? Yes, he could!

Franklin invented the **armonica**.

The armonica had glass bowls. Each bowl was a different size. The bowls went on a metal rod. Franklin pushed a pedal to turn the bowls. Then he touched them with wet fingers.

Each bowl made a different sound!

Benjamin Franklin was in charge of the mail system.
He wanted the mail to be delivered faster.

Franklin invented the **odometer** to help find the shortest
ways to get to places.
An odometer measures distance.
Franklin put the odometer on a carriage wheel.
The odometer counted how many times the wheel turned.
One mile was 400 turns of the wheel.
A bell rang to mark the miles.

Benjamin Franklin loved to read.
But his eyes did not work well.
He needed one pair of glasses to see things close up. He needed another pair to see things far away.

Franklin got tired of changing his glasses. What could he do?

He invented **bifocal glasses**. Bifocals have two pieces of glass in each frame. One piece of glass helps people see things that are close. The other piece helps people see things that are far away.

People still wear Franklin's invention today.

Benjamin Franklin spent many hours in his library. He had shelves filled with books. Some books were hard to reach.
How could he reach the books?

He looked at a chair in his library.
He had an idea! He added steps to the chair. The steps could fold back into the chair. The chair could be a ladder or a chair.

Franklin invented the library chair.

Benjamin Franklin was a very smart scientist.
He was a clever inventor.
He loved reading, thinking and learning all of his life.

Franklin died in Philadelphia, USA on 17 April, 1790.

Timeline

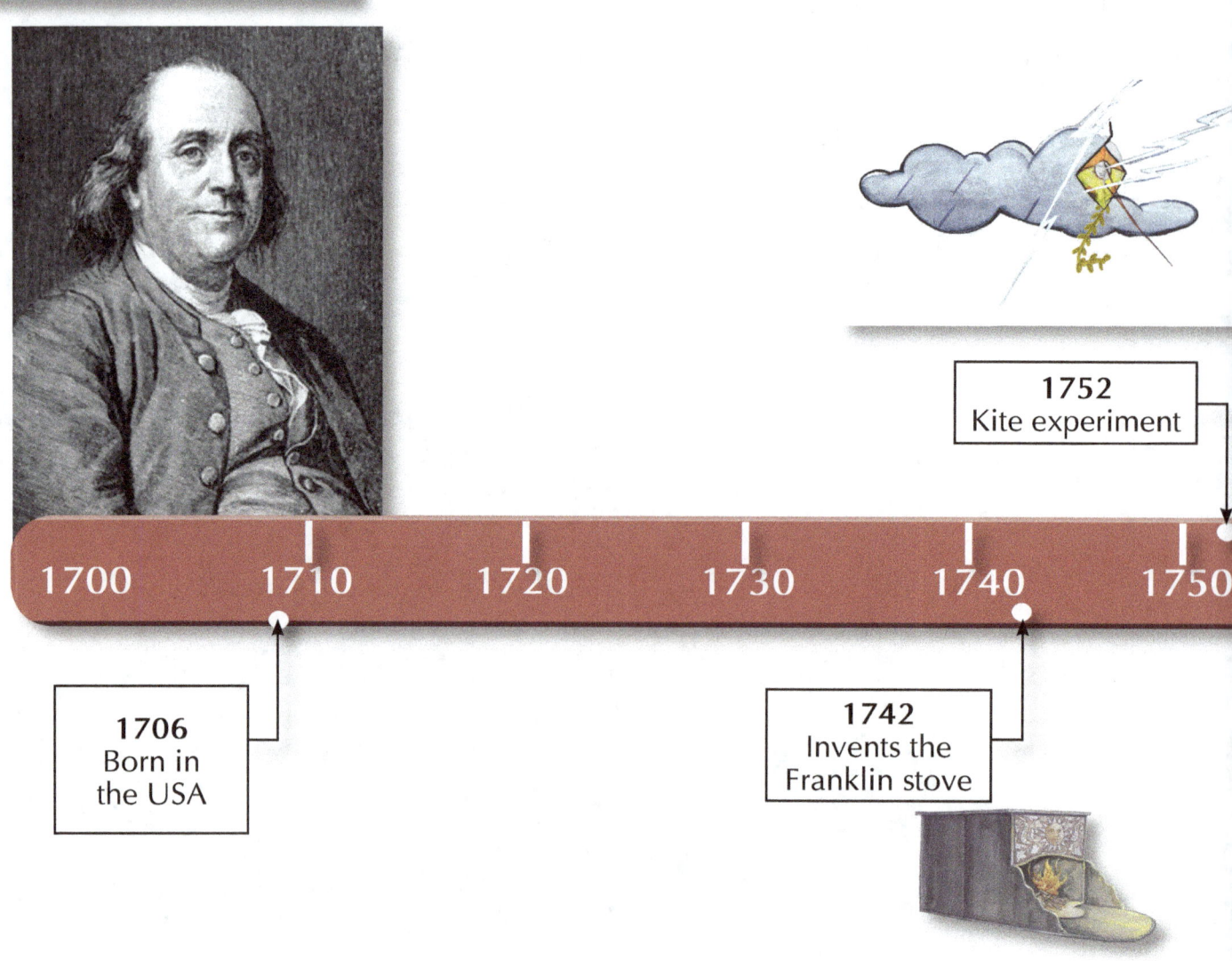

1752
Kite experiment

1700   1710   1720   1730   1740   1750

1706
Born in
the USA

1742
Invents the
Franklin stove

Benjamin Franklin's Life and Work

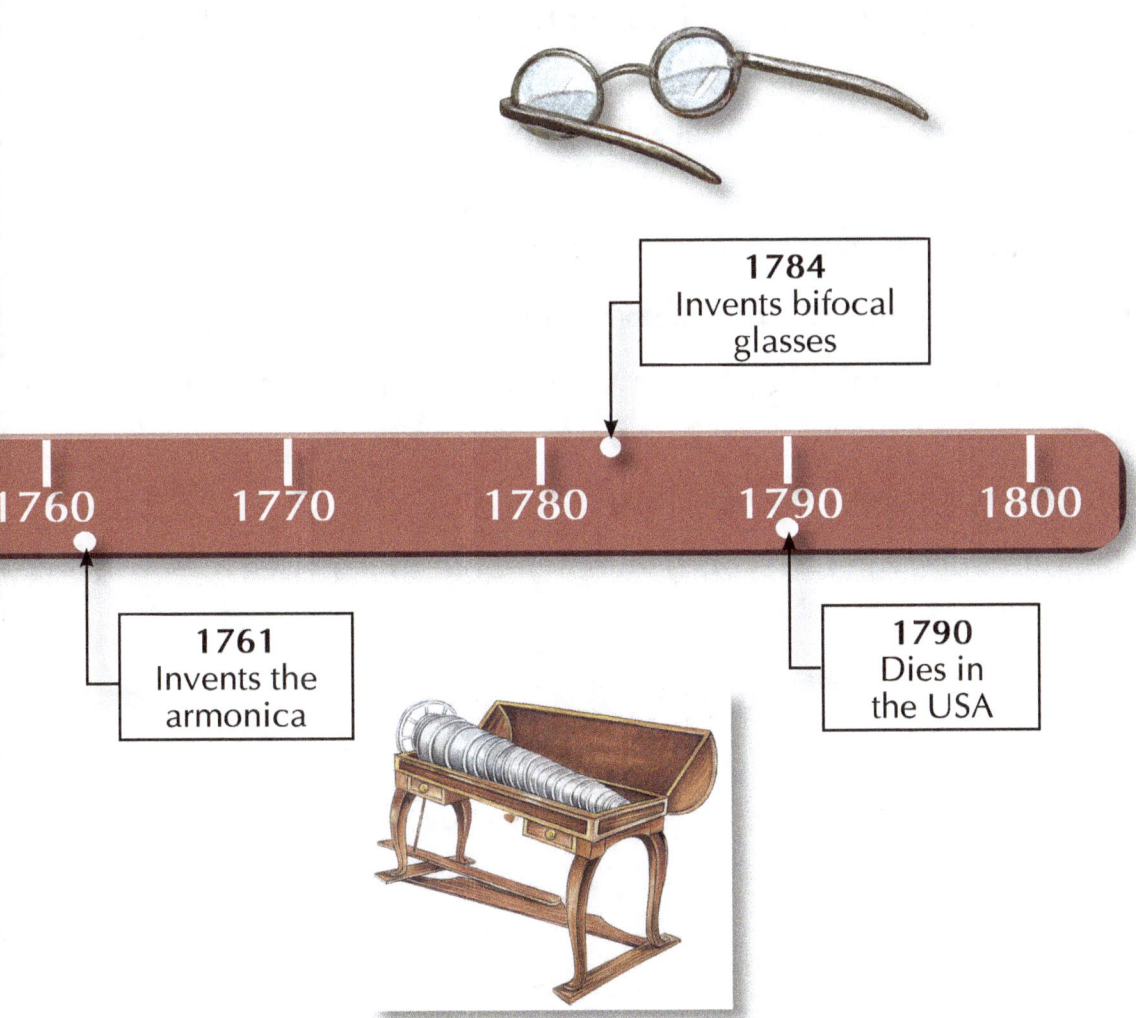

1784
Invents bifocal
glasses

1760   1770   1780   1790   1800

1761
Invents the
armonica

1790
Dies in
the USA

Word Meanings

Armonica: A musical instrument that has glass bowls

Bifocal Glasses: Glasses with lenses that are divided into two parts. The upper half is for looking far away things and the lower half is for looking at things that are near

Electricity: Energy that can be used to make light and heat. Lightning is a form of electricity

Franklin Stove: An iron stove that helps heat a room well

Inventor: Someone who designs or creates something that did not exist before

Lightning Rod: A piece of metal that goes on top of a building to protect it from lightning

Odometer: A tool that measures distance traveled

USA: The third largest country in the world, located in North America

Think, Talk and Write

Think About It

Look at the book again.

Use a bookmark to mark the invention you like best.

Think about why you liked it best.

Draw the invention you liked best. Use pictures in the book to help you.

Talk About It

Share your drawing with friends or family.

Tell them why you think it is an important invention.

Tell them about Benjamin Franklin's other inventions.

Ask which one they like best.

Ask what they know about Franklin.

Write About It

Franklin was always thinking about new things to invent. What would you like to invent?

Make a drawing of your invention. Write a few sentences that describe it.

What did you learn from Benjamin Franklin?

....

....

....

....

....

....

....

....

....

....

....

....

....

....

What are the five things that you will change after reading Benjamin Franklin's story?

....

....

....

....

....

....

....

....

....

....

....

....

....

....

A Day With

Louis Pasteur

Louis Pasteur saved millions of lives.
How did he help to prevent many diseases?
Read on to discover the answer.

Meet Tim and Tyra

Hi, I'm Tim.

Hi, I'm Tyra. We are going to travel back in time to visit Louis Pasteur. Let's meet him now.

Chapter 1: In Louis Pasteur's Lab

Hi, Mr Pasteur.

Hello, Tim. Hello, Tyra. Welcome to my lab. I'd like to tell you about my life and show you some of the things I've done.

Hello, Mr Pasteur.

Louis Pasteur was born in Dole, France on 27 December, 1822.

He was a scientist and **biologist**.

He invented a new science called **microbiology**.

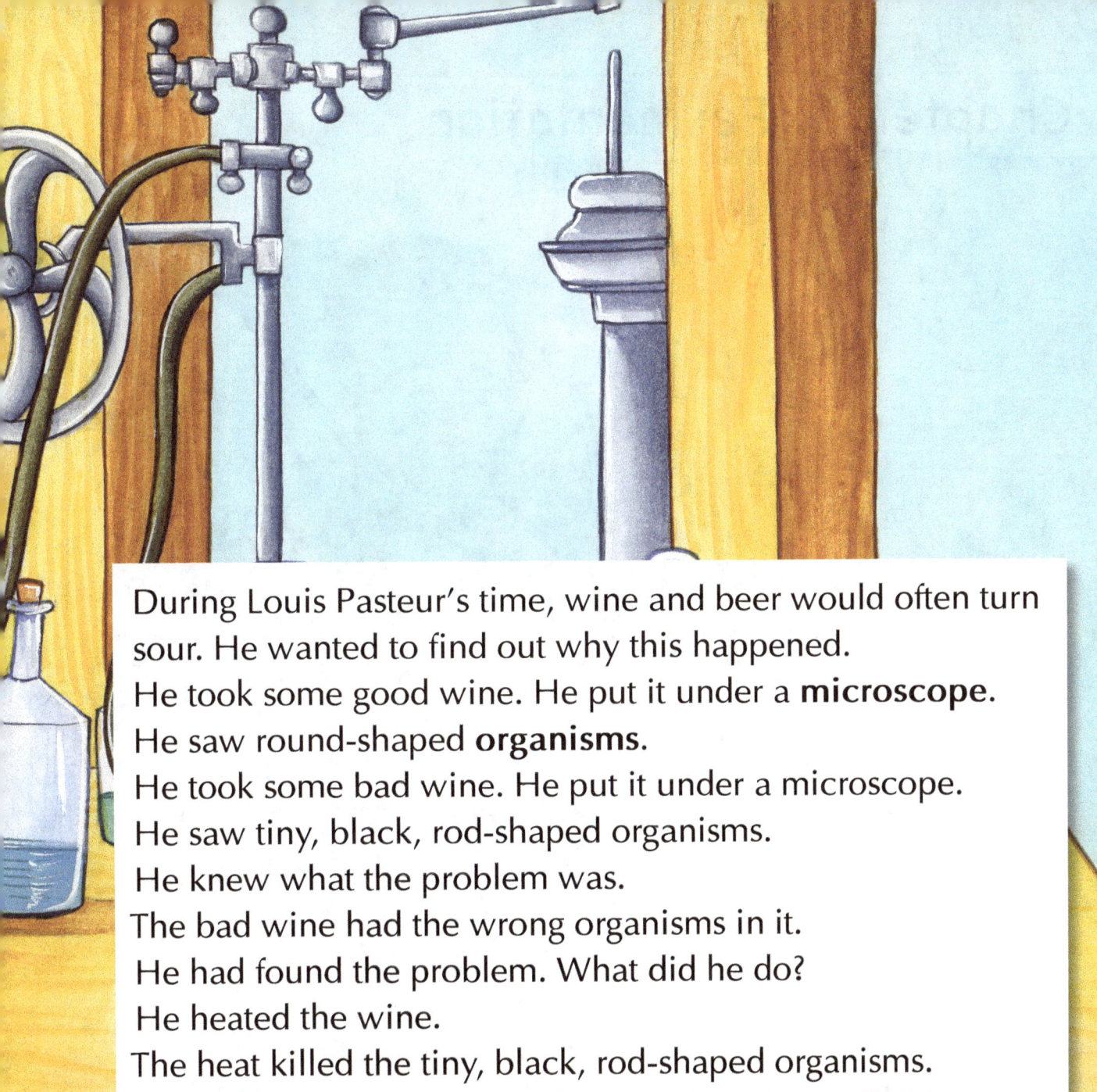

During Louis Pasteur's time, wine and beer would often turn sour. He wanted to find out why this happened.

He took some good wine. He put it under a **microscope**.

He saw round-shaped **organisms**.

He took some bad wine. He put it under a microscope.

He saw tiny, black, rod-shaped organisms.

He knew what the problem was.

The bad wine had the wrong organisms in it.

He had found the problem. What did he do?

He heated the wine.

The heat killed the tiny, black, rod-shaped organisms.

Wine is made by **fermentation**.
Louis Pasteur knew that **yeast** made things ferment.
But no one knew how it happened.

Pasteur wanted to find out.
He took a sample of wine.
He looked into his microscope.
He was surprised! The yeast was alive.
He saw it grow and divide.
He saw it give off **alcohol** and a gas.
Now he knew how fermentation happened.

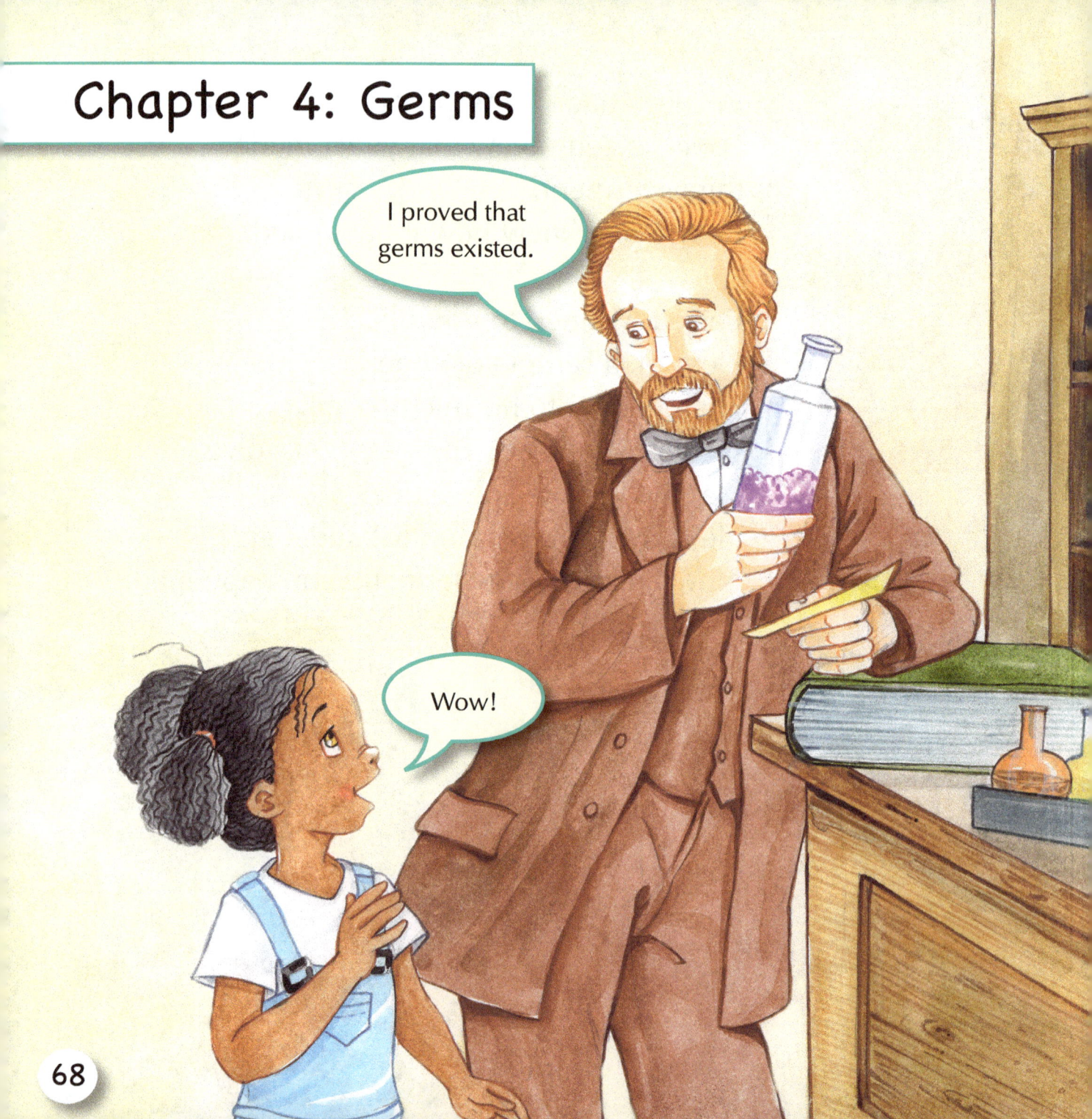

Louis Pasteur liked to do **research**.
He proved that **germs** existed.
He also proved that germs carried diseases.
This became known as the "germ theory" of disease.

Chapter 5: Pasteurization

Pasteur did a lot of research.
He learned that **bacteria** spoiled milk. They also caused diseases.
He heated the milk. He looked through his microscope.
The heat had killed the bacteria.
He heated other liquids. The heat killed the bacteria.
Heating food to kill bacteria became known as pasteurization.

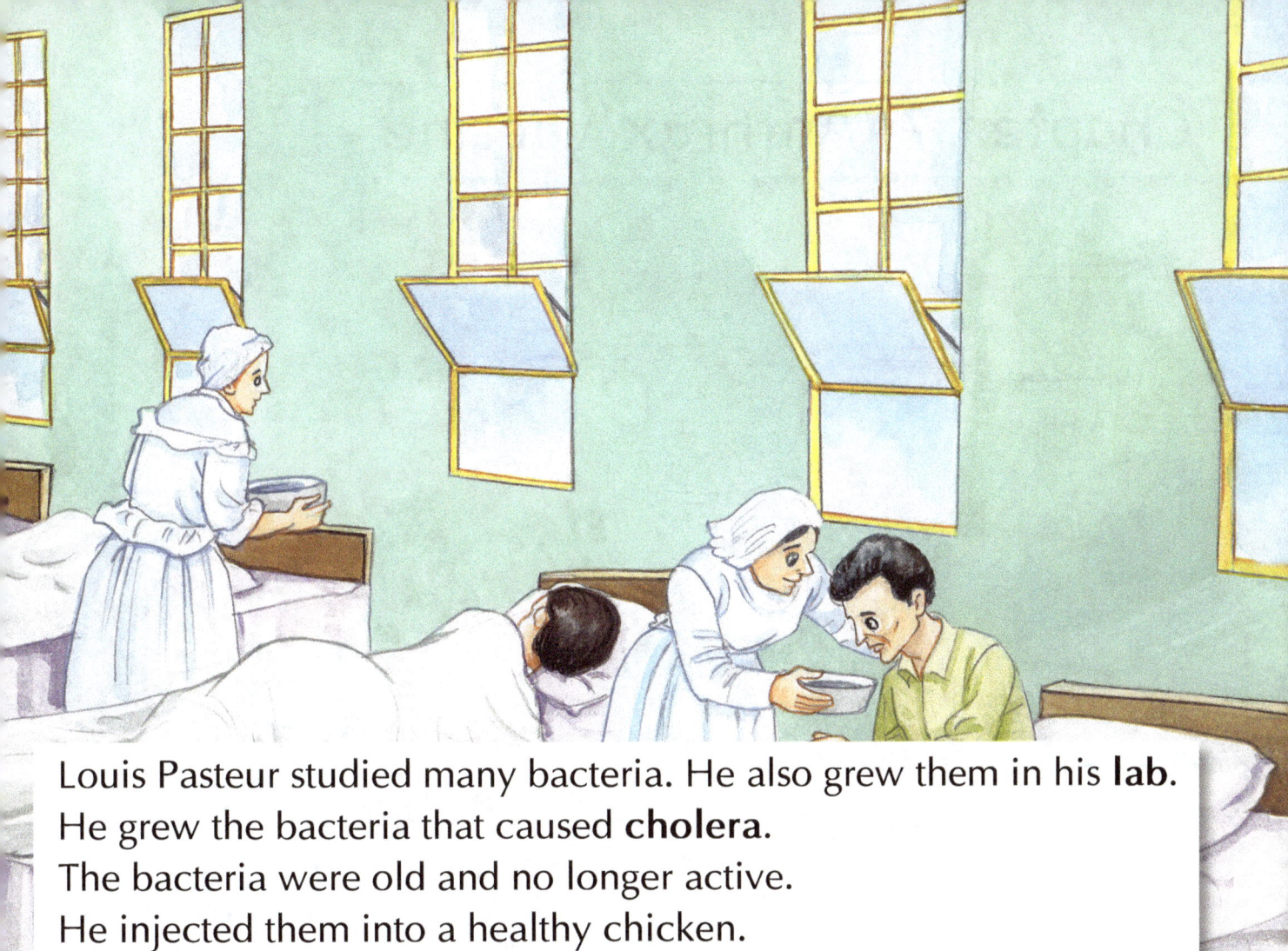

Louis Pasteur studied many bacteria. He also grew them in his **lab**.
He grew the bacteria that caused **cholera**.
The bacteria were old and no longer active.
He injected them into a healthy chicken.
What happened? The chicken did not fall sick with cholera.
He found that the weak bacteria acted as a **vaccine**.
The chicken would no longer be infected by cholera.
He had discovered vaccine. It was a great discovery.
He cured many people with his vaccine.

Louis Pasteur studied anthrax. Anthrax was a disease that killed many animals. It was caused by bacteria. It also infected people. He worked to find a vaccine for anthrax.
First, he had to weaken the anthrax bacteria.
He did many experiments.
Finally, he produced weak and harmless anthrax bacteria.
He tested his vaccine on cattle and sheep. It worked!
He discovered a vaccine for anthrax.

At that time, rabies was a common disease in France.
Many people died. Louis Pasteur wanted to find a vaccine for rabies.
He studied animals that had rabies. Soon he produced a vaccine.
He first tested his vaccine on animals.
He then tested his vaccine on a boy.
The boy was bitten by a rabid dog. The boy did not develop rabies.
Pasteur discovered a vaccine for rabies.

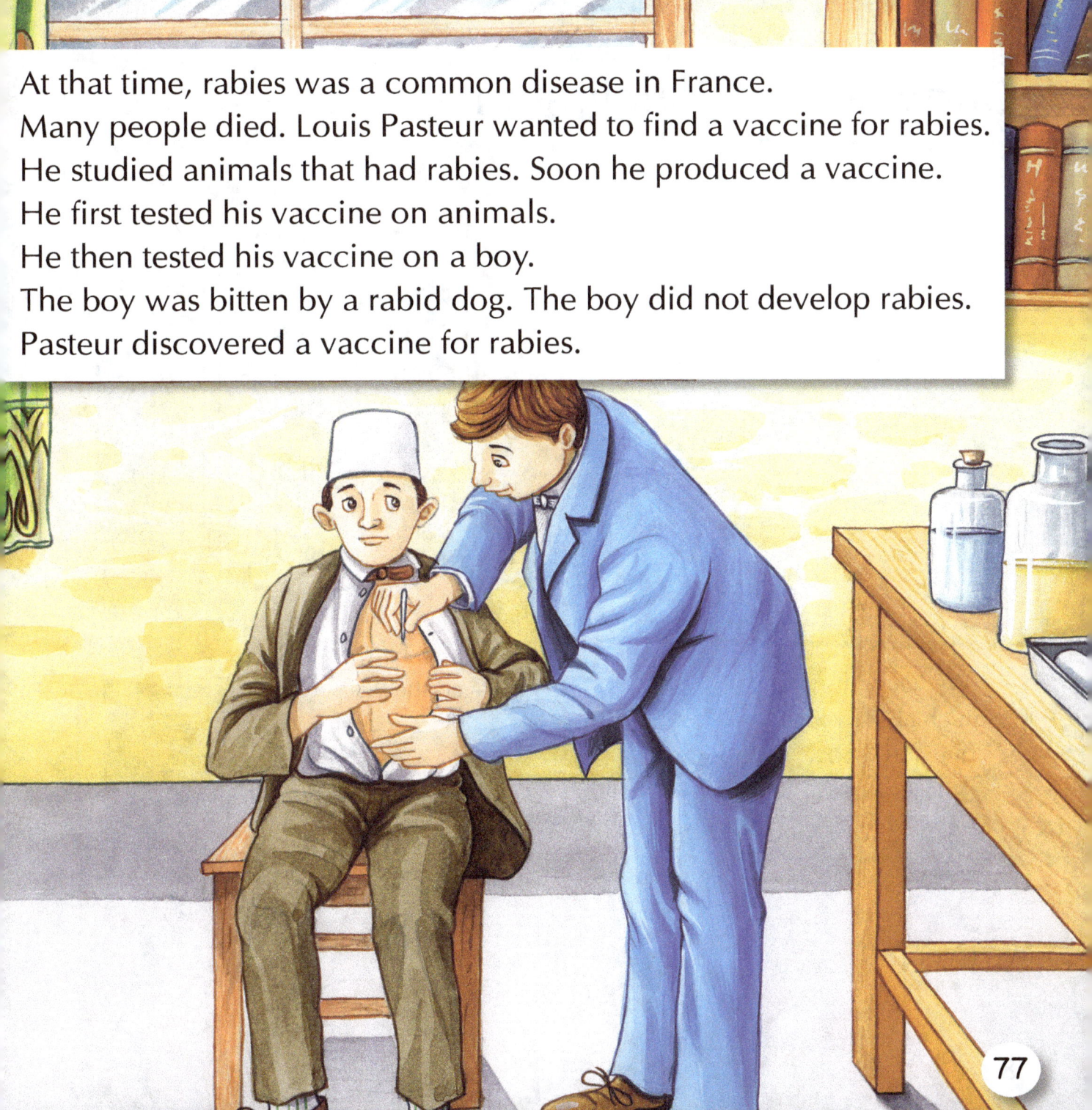

Chapter 9: Conclusion

Louis Pasteur was a great scientist.
He taught people how to fight diseases.
Pasteur Institutes were built all over the world to fight diseases.
It was a great **honour** for a great man.

Pasteur died in Marnes-la-Coquette, France on 28 September, 1895.

1857
Discovers
fermentation

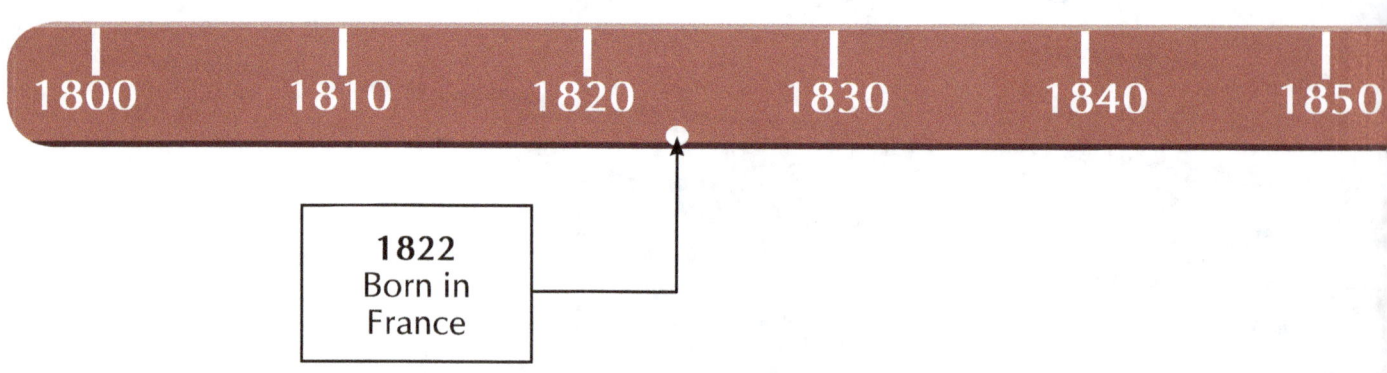

1800   1810   1820   1830   1840   1850

1822
Born in
France

Louis Pasteur's Life and Work

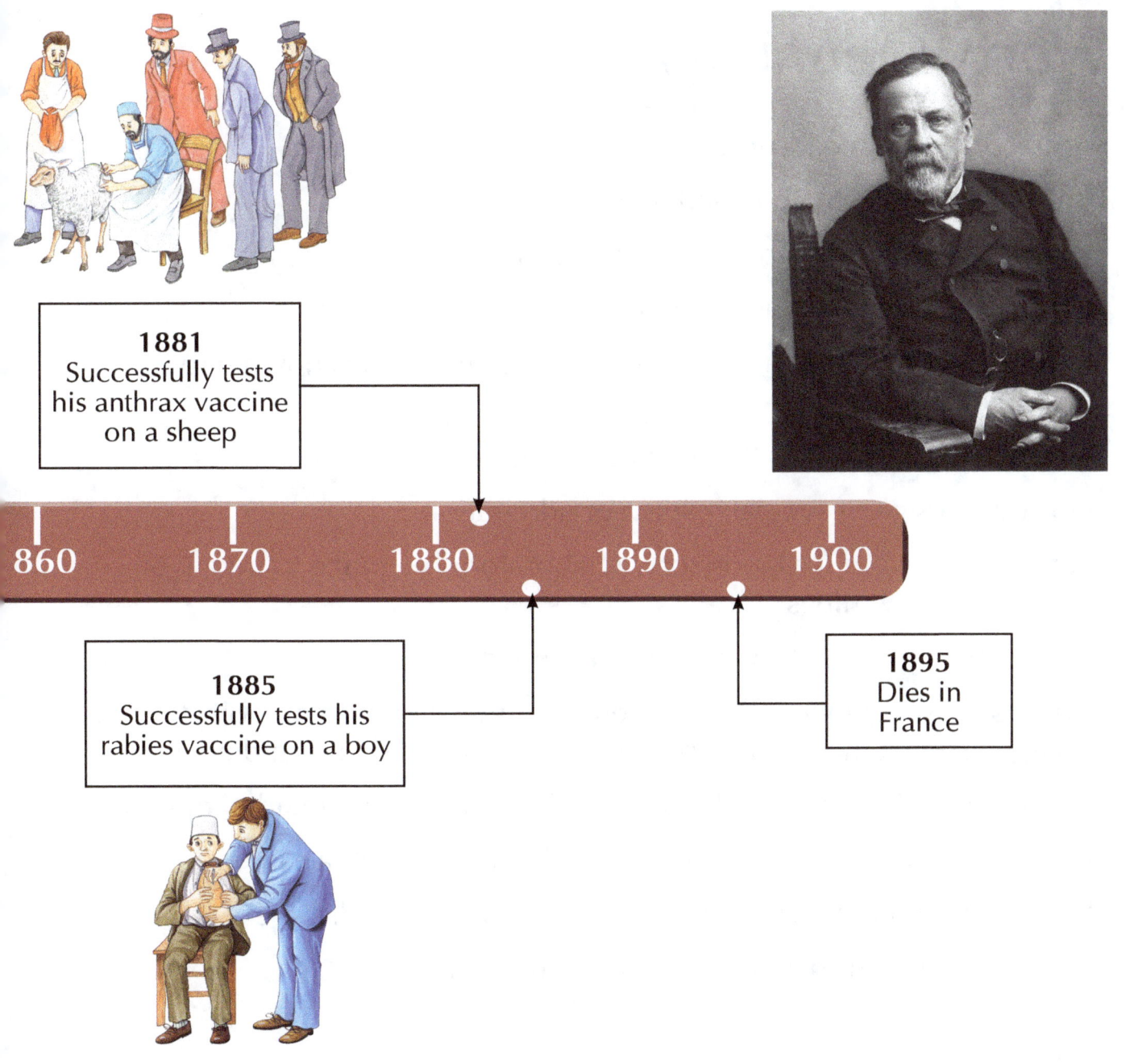

1881
Successfully tests
his anthrax vaccine
on a sheep

860 1870 1880 1890 1900

1885
Successfully tests his
rabies vaccine on a boy

1895
Dies in
France

Word Meanings

Alcohol: A chemical substance

Bacteria: Small, single-celled germs

Biologist: A person who studies organisms

Cholera: A disease caused by bacteria

Fermentation: A process in which a substance breaks down into simpler substances

Germs: Tiny organisms that can cause diseases

Honour: A sign of special respect or admiration

Lab: A short word for laboratory. A laboratory is a place to invent or discover new things

Microbiology: The study of germs or tiny organisms

Microscope: A device that uses lenses to make very small objects look larger, so that they can be scientifically examined and studied

Organisms: Tiny forms of life that are invisible to the unaided eye

Research: To study something thoroughly to find out facts

Vaccine: A medicine that is given to help prevent a disease

Yeast: Tiny organisms that cause fermentation

Think, Talk and Write

What did Louis Pasteur learn about germs?
Do you think germs are dangerous? Why or why not?
Which discovery did you find the most interesting? Why?

Talk About It

Work with a partner. Talk about the many diseases that are caused
by tiny organisms.
Work together to make a list of the diseases.

Write About It

Louis Pasteur wanted to learn about diseases.
What disease would you like to learn about?
Write a few sentences telling what disease you would like to learn
more about and why.

What did you learn from Louis Pasteur?

What are the five things that you will change after reading Louis Pasteur's story?

....

....

....

....

....

....

....

....

....

....

....

....

....

....

Thomas Alva Edison

Thomas Alva Edison invented things that changed the world.
What were these great inventions?
Why were these inventions so important?
Read on to discover the answer.

Meet Tim and Tyra

Hi, I'm Tim.

Hi, I'm Tyra. We are going to travel back in time to visit Thomas Alva Edison. Let's meet him now.

Thomas Alva Edison was born in Milan, USA on 11 February,1847.
Edison was a great scientist and inventor.

Young Thomas Edison wanted to learn about science.
He set up his own science lab. He was only 10.
The science lab was in his basement.
He did many experiments there.

Thomas Edison had a friend. His name was Jim.
Edison and Jim made their own **telegraph**.
A telegraph sends messages. It uses a **code**.
The boys sent messages to each other.

Later, Edison got a job. He worked for a company
that sent telegraph messages.
Edison was very fast at sending messages.
He was the fastest worker at the telegraph company.

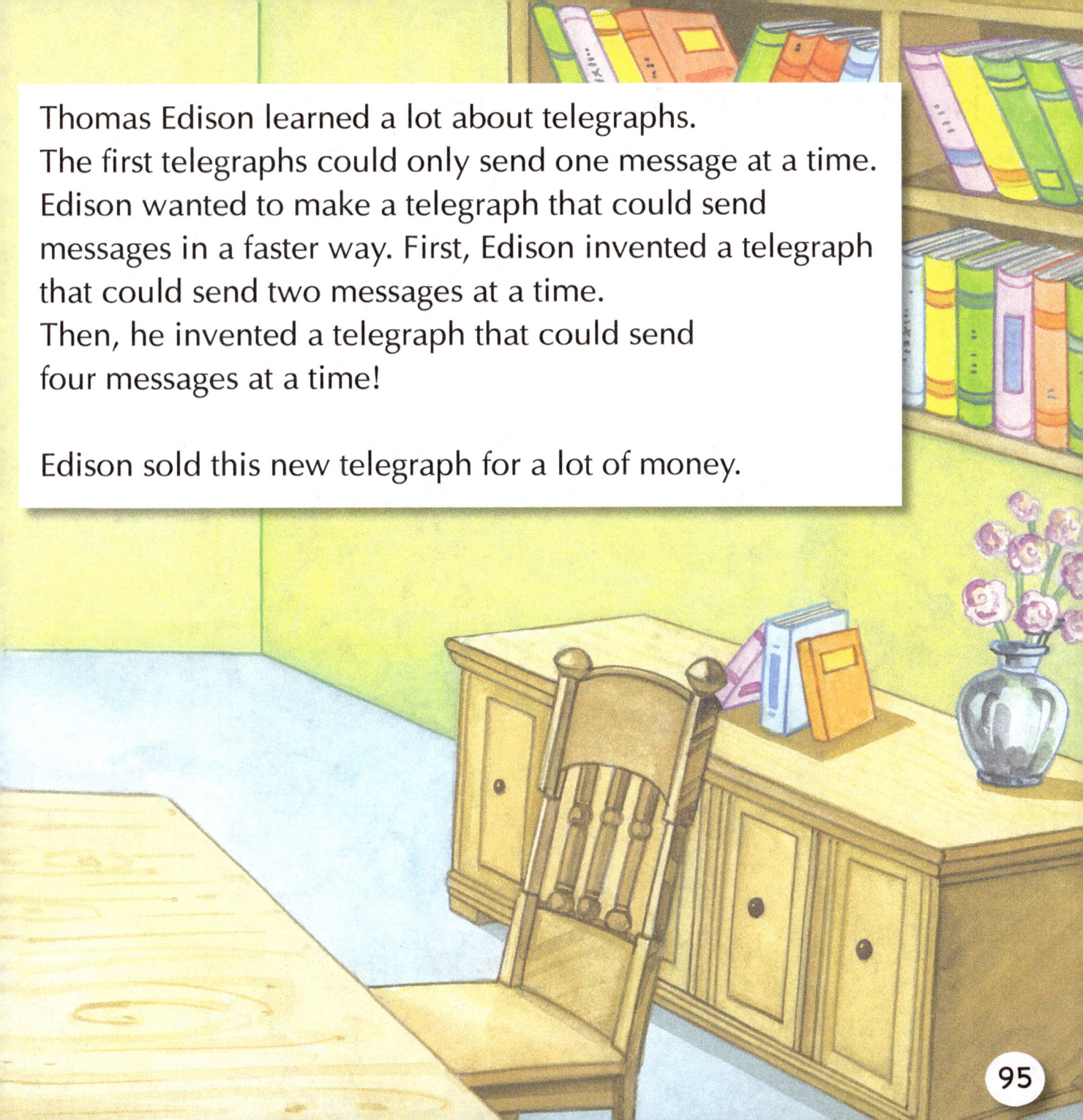

Thomas Edison learned a lot about telegraphs.
The first telegraphs could only send one message at a time.
Edison wanted to make a telegraph that could send
messages in a faster way. First, Edison invented a telegraph
that could send two messages at a time.
Then, he invented a telegraph that could send
four messages at a time!

Edison sold this new telegraph for a lot of money.

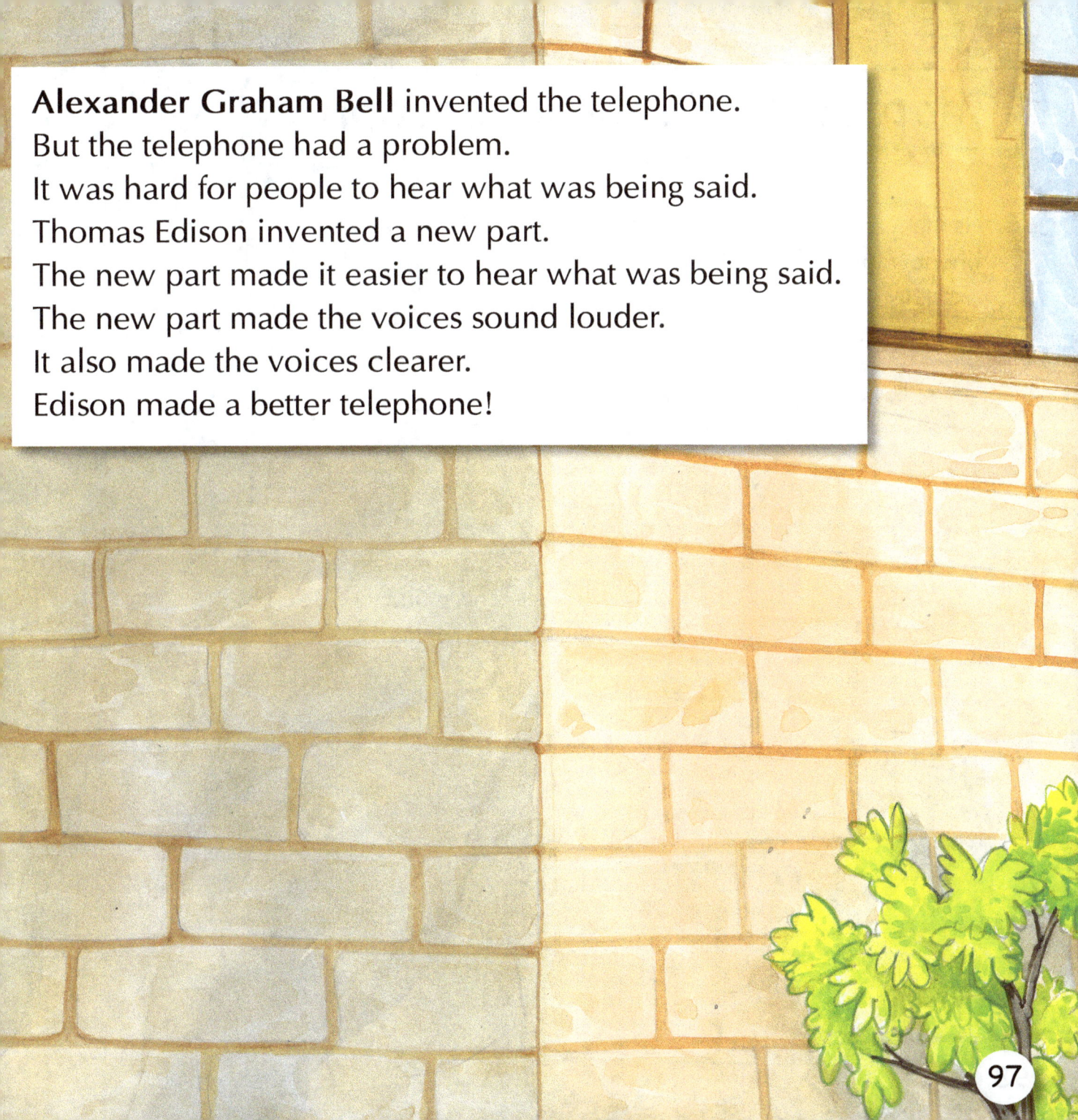

Alexander Graham Bell invented the telephone.
But the telephone had a problem.
It was hard for people to hear what was being said.
Thomas Edison invented a new part.
The new part made it easier to hear what was being said.
The new part made the voices sound louder.
It also made the voices clearer.
Edison made a better telephone!

Thomas Edison used what he learned about telephones to invent a talking machine. He called it the **phonograph**. It could **record** sounds and then play them for people to hear.

Edison spoke the first words ever recorded with a phonograph. His words were, "Mary had a little lamb." The phonograph was one of Edison's favorite inventions.

In the 1870s, most people used candles or special lamps to light their homes.
These lamps used gas or oil.
They were not very safe.
They could start fires.

Thomas Edison wanted to invent a safer kind of light.
There were **electric** light bulbs, but they did not work very well.
The light bulbs did not stay bright for very long.
Edison wanted to make a better light bulb.

He worked for more than a year. What happened?
Thomas Edison found a way to make a light bulb with a special kind of cotton thread inside.
When electricity went through the thread, it glowed.
The light bulb stayed bright for a long time.
Edison invented a better light bulb.

Soon, many people wanted Edison's light bulbs.

Thomas Edison invented a **movie camera**.
He made a machine to show movies.
It had an **eyepiece** on top. Just one person
at a time could look through the eyepiece and see
the movie.

Edison started a movie company. He made many movies.

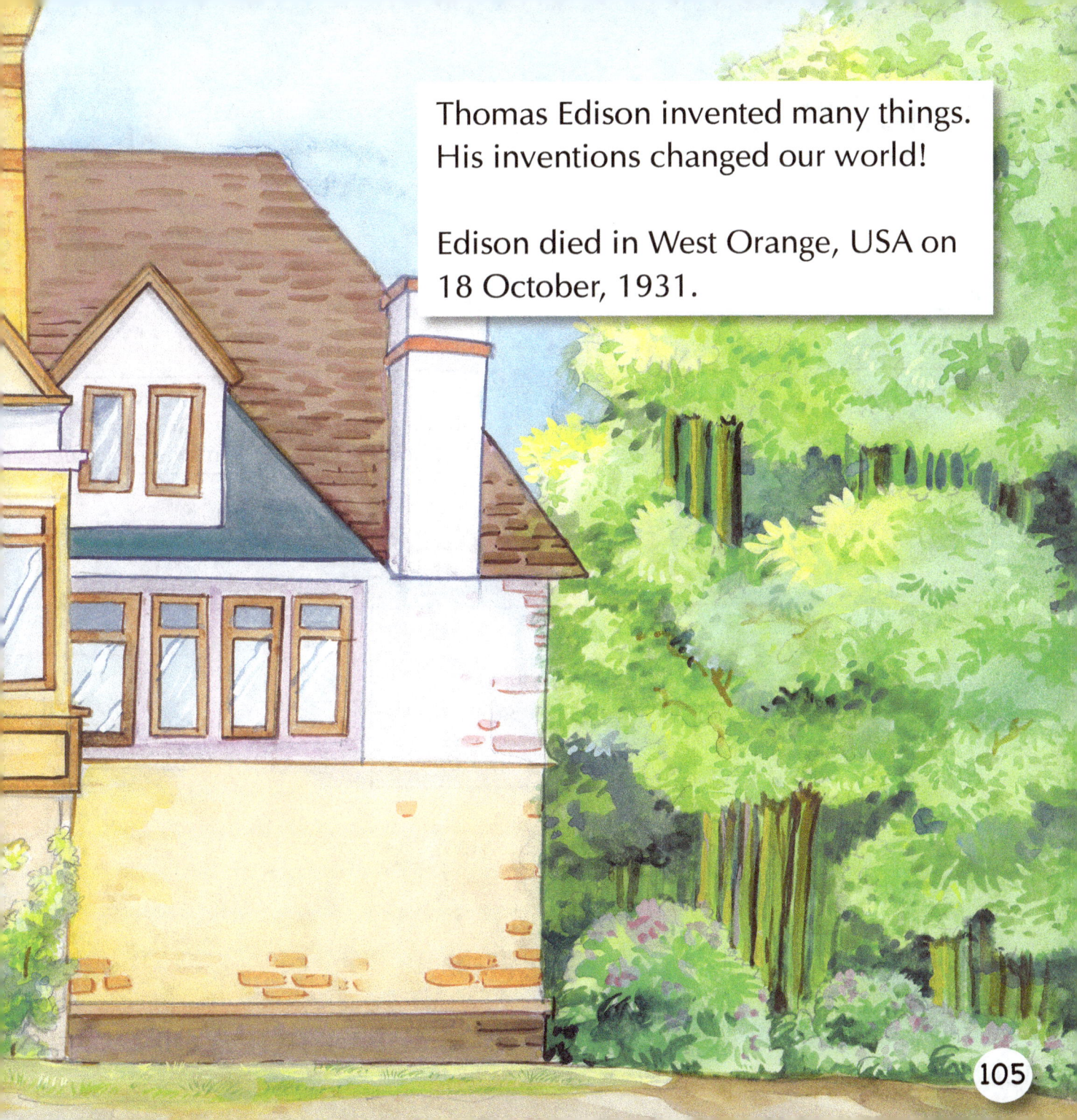

Thomas Edison invented many things.
His inventions changed our world!

Edison died in West Orange, USA on
18 October, 1931.

Timeline

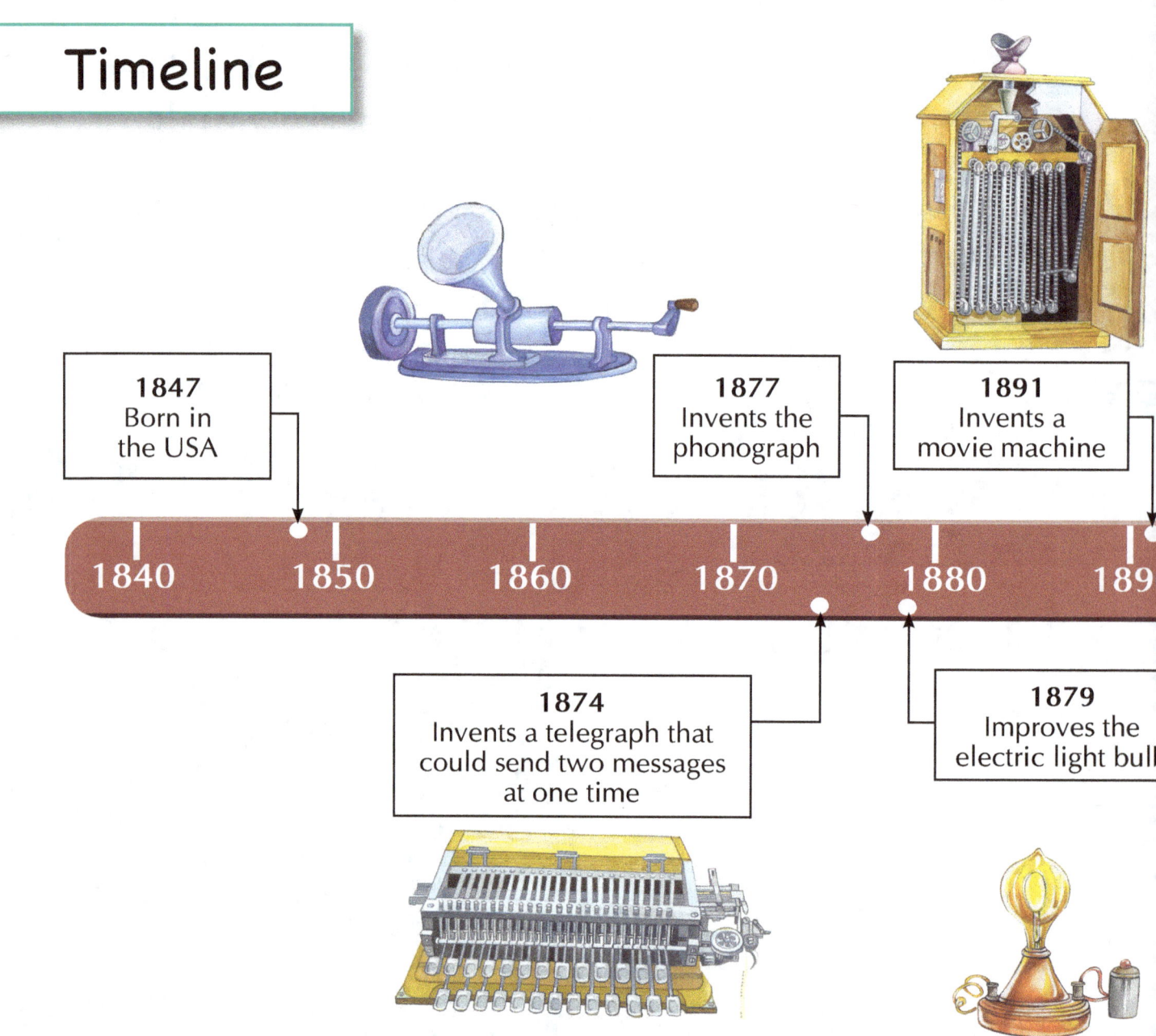

1847
Born in
the USA

1877
Invents the
phonograph

1891
Invents a
movie machine

1840 1850 1860 1870 1880 1890

1874
Invents a telegraph that
could send two messages
at one time

1879
Improves the
electric light bulb

Thomas Alva Edison's Life and Work

1900   1910   1920   1930   1940

1931
Dies in the USA

Word Meanings

Alexander Graham Bell: Scottish inventor who invented the first telephone

Electric: Something that uses electricity

Eyepiece: A thing to look through and see something

Code: A secret or hidden way of sending messages

Movie Camera: A machine that takes pictures that make movies

Phonograph: A machine that makes recorded sound

Record: To put sound on a tape or a CD

Telegraph: A machine that uses electricity to send messages in code

Think, Talk and Write

Think About It

Thomas Alva Edison made some of the first movies.
Think about a movie you would like to make.
What is your movie about?
Make a poster that shows your movie idea.

Talk About It

Work with a partner.
Talk about why you think Edison's electric light bulb was important.
Work together to make a list of your reasons.

Write About It

Think about something you use everyday.
How can this object be better? What would you like it to do?
Edison made a better light bulb. Write about how your object can be better too.

What did you learn from Thomas Alva Edison?

....

....

....

....

....

....

....

....

....

....

....

....

....

What are the five things that you will change after reading Thomas Alva Edison's story?

....

....

....

....

....

....

....

....

....

....

....

....

....

....

Work Space

www.ingramcontent.com/pod-product-compliance
Lightning Source LLC
Chambersburg PA
CBHW080959020726
47505CB00009B/2259